Josie
and
Mr. Fernandez

Please visit our web site at: www.garethstevens.com
For a free color catalog describing Gareth Stevens Publishing's
list of high-quality books and multimedia programs, call
1-800-542-2595 or fax your request to (414) 332-3567.

Library of Congress Cataloging-in-Publication Data

Backx, Patsy.
    [Fientje en Meneer Fernandez. English]
    Josie and Mr. Fernandez / by Patsy Backx.
        p. cm.
    Summary: After Josie bumps into a man and spills the groceries he is carrying,
a nearby dog eats some of his cookies, so he buys a new bag to share with Josie.
    ISBN 0-8368-3079-2 (lib. bdg.)
    [1. Cookies—Fiction. 2. Dogs—Fiction.] I. Title.
PZ7.B132375Jo   2002
[E]—dc21
                                                        2001054218

This North American edition first published in 2002 by
Gareth Stevens Publishing
A World Almanac Education Group Company
330 West Olive Street, Suite 100
Milwaukee, Wisconsin 53212 USA

This U.S. edition © 2002 by Gareth Stevens, Inc. Text and illustrations
© 1999 by Patsy Backx. Original edition published as *Fientje en Meneer
Fernandez* © J.H. Gottmer/H.J.W. Becht bv, The Netherlands.

Gareth Stevens cover design: Eva Erato-Rudek
Gareth Stevens editor: Dorothy L. Gibbs

Printed in the United States of America

1 2 3 4 5 6 7 8 9 06 05 04 03 02

Josie
and
Mr. Fernandez

by Patsy Backx

Gareth Stevens Publishing
A WORLD ALMANAC EDUCATION GROUP COMPANY

Josie had a brand new scooter,
a red one with a bell on it.
She rode it all around the town.
And she could go very fast!

One day, Josie was riding her scooter very fast along the river.

When she got to the bridge,
she zoomed across it like a rocket.

She didn't see the man on the other side
until — THUMP! — too late.

The man was wearing a dark gray coat
and a little black hat, and he had a
black mustache. It was Mr. Fernandez!
He had been carrying a bag of groceries.

Now his groceries were scattered
all over the street. He looked very angry.
"I'm sorry," said Josie, in a quiet voice.
"Look at this mess!" shouted Mr. Fernandez.

There were groceries everywhere —
coffee, tea, butter, oatmeal, some matches
and toilet paper, a bar of soap, a bottle of
juice, a loaf of bread, a candy bar, and
a bag of cookies.

Josie helped Mr. Fernandez pick up
all the groceries and put them back
into the bag — except the cookies.

14

The bag of cookies was lying
on the ground, hidden near a tree.
Josie didn't see it until — TOO LATE!
Mr. Fernandez and his groceries
were already gone.

Josie jumped onto her scooter
and rode very fast down the street.
She wanted to catch Mr. Fernandez
and return his bag of cookies.

But, at the very first corner, a big, brown dog with sharp, white teeth made Josie stop. The dog was staring straight at the cookies.

The big dog growled and snarled as
it moved closer and closer to the cookies.
Josie was shaking. She was so scared.
"What shall I do?" she wondered.

Finally, Josie decided. She gave
the cookies to the big, scary dog,
and — CHOMP! — he gobbled them
up — every last one of them!

Just then, Mr. Fernandez came
around the corner. He was bent over,
looking everywhere on the ground for
his bag of cookies.

"Hello, Josie," he said calmly. "Have
you seen my cookies? I can't find
them anywhere." Josie looked at
Mr. Fernandez, with tears in her eyes.

"I saw your cookies," she replied,
"but —" She pointed at the big,
brown dog. "You won't find
your cookies now," she said.
"That big dog ate them all!"

Mr. Fernandez shook his finger at the dog. "Bad dog!" he said, in a very stern voice. The big dog huddled down close to the ground, looking very ashamed.

Mr. Fernandez turned back to Josie.
"I have a little money left," he said.
"So I will buy some more cookies.
Would you like to come along?"

Josie hopped onto her scooter and
followed Mr. Fernandez to the store.
Mr. Fernandez bought a giant bag of
cookies — at least a pound and a half!

There were all sorts of cookies in the bag, all the kinds Josie liked best. Together, Josie and Mr. Fernandez gobbled them up — every last one of them!

31